Sharing Books From Birth to Five

Welcome to Practical Parenting Books

It's never too early to introduce a child to books. It's wonderful to see your baby gazing intently at a cloth book; your toddler poring over a favourite picture; or your older child listening quietly to a story. And you're his favourite storyteller, so have fun together while you're reading – use silly voices, linger over the pictures and leave pauses for your child to join in.

Meet Jessie and Joe, their family and friends, in *The Piggy Race*. They live on Little Oak Farm, a busy farm that's open to visitors. Enjoy the excitement of the first piggy race of the year and choose your own favourite pigs! Chat about the meaning of friendship and how to make up after a quarrel. Look at the map together, talk about the animals and, if you can, visit an open farm yourselves.

Books open doors to other worlds, so take a few minutes out of your busy day to cuddle up close and lose yourselves in a story. Your child will love it – and so will you.

Jane & Clare

Jane Kemp   Clare Walters

P.S. Look out, too, for *Rocket To The Rescue*, the companion book in this age range, and all the other great books in the new Practical Parenting series.

AGE
3-5

First published in Great Britain by HarperCollins Publishers Ltd in 2000

3 5 7 9 8 6 4 2

ISBN: 0-00-136153-8

Text copyright © Jane Kemp and Clare Walters 2000
Illustrations copyright © Anthony Lewis 2000

The Practical Parenting/HarperCollins pre-school book series has been created by Jane Kemp and Clare Walters.
The Practical Parenting imprimatur is used with permission by IPC Magazines Ltd.

Practical Parenting is published monthly by IPC Magazines Ltd. For subscription enquiries
and orders ring 01444 445555 or the credit card hotline (UK orders only) on 01622 778778.

The HarperCollins website address is: www.fireandwater.com

Printed in Hong Kong by Printing Express Limited

Little Oak Farm

The Piggy Race

Written by Jane Kemp and Clare Walters

Illustrated by Anthony Lewis

Collins

An imprint of HarperCollinsPublishers

Jessie and her brother Joe live on Little Oak Farm. There's always lots to do because every afternoon their farm is open for visitors.

It was one of Jessie and Joe's favourite days – the first Piggy Race of the year at Little Oak Farm.

"Do you like my piggies, Jessie?" asked Joe, as they were finishing off the big poster for the visitors' ticket office.

"Mine are better," boasted Jessie.

"Joe's pigs look fine to me," said Dad, "Come on – time to choose which pig you want to win."

Jessie raced to get to the pig pen first.

"I'm going to get the best pig," she shouted.

"It's not fair!" said Joe, feeling tearful. "You always win races."

"Well, I'm bigger," replied Jessie.

"I'm having Curly," announced Jessie.

"She's got the twistiest tail."

"I'll have Titch," said Joe quietly,

"he's small, like me."

TITCH

SHADES CHAMPION SPOTT TANK

Dad had brought out the paint pots and was painting
a different coloured spot on each pig's back so that
the visitors would know which pig was which.

"Does that hurt them?" asked Joe.

"Oh, no," said Dad. "The pigs don't notice it and the
paint washes off very easily."

"Do pigs like running, Dad?" asked Jessie.

"They certainly do," replied Dad, "especially as there's some delicious pig food at the end of the track – and you know how pigs love to eat."

"I like eating, too," said Joe, "is it lunchtime yet?"

"We've got work to do first," laughed Dad.

"Mind out, Rocket," said Dad as Jessie and Joe helped him
to clean out the pen, put food in the trough and bring
fresh water in buckets.

After lunch the farm visitors began to arrive. Suddenly, one little girl started shouting at the top of her voice.

"Why is that girl so noisy, Mum?" asked Jessie.

"I expect she's just excited to be at Little Oak Farm," replied Mum.

Jessie, Joe and Mum started to take all the children
to the Fun Room. They were going to make rosettes
for the Piggy Race.

Suddenly a voice shouted, "I want an ice cream!"
It was the little girl again.

"There's no need to make such a noise, Lucy," said the
girl's mum crossly. "We'll have one later. You're going to
make a rosette now."

Soon the rosettes were nearly ready.

"My colour's red because I'm supporting Titch,"
explained Joe, making an extra rosette for luck.

"And I'm blue. I want Curly to win," said Jessie.

"Which pig have you chosen, Lucy?" Jessie asked.

"The big pig, Champion," answered Lucy, "because the biggest always wins. And yellow's my favourite colour."

Jessie wasn't sure she liked Lucy.

As everyone waited for the race to begin, Jessie and Lucy began their own Piggy Race around the Play Barn.

"I'm Curly, I'm winning!" yelled Jessie.

"I'm Champion, and *I'm* winning!" shouted Lucy.

"I'll crawl through this tunnel," thought Joe, and he popped out in time to beat them both.

"I won! I won!" he shouted happily.

"But you cheated!" accused Jessie.

"No I didn't," said poor Joe, and he started to cry.

Lucy suddenly felt sorry for him. "Don't be sad, Joe," she said.

"I never win," sniffed Joe. "And I bet Titch won't win the Piggy Race either."

"He might if we *both* cheer for him," said Lucy. "I don't really mind about Champion." And she kindly took off her yellow rosette and put on one of Joe's red ones instead.

Joe felt much happier.

"LITTLE OAK FARM VISITORS!" came Dad's voice over
the loudspeaker. "THE PIGGY RACE IS ABOUT
TO BEGIN!"

"Come on!" said Jessie. "Let's all find a good place
to watch."

As the visitors sat down, Wilf put out the pig food.

START

"Everyone choose your favourite pig!" called Old Alfred, carrying a large board with all the pigs' names on it. He'd already chosen, Champion. Mum was supporting Spotty, and Katie the cook liked Shades, the big-eared pig. Tankerman Fred chose Tank, of course.

"Wake up, pigs!" shouted Dad. "Everyone join in… *one, two, three*, wake up piggies!"

"WAKE UP PIGGIES!" they all called.

"Ready, Steady, Go!"

Wilf opened the door and the six pigs ran out and streaked off towards the food by the finishing line.

Everyone cheered, but Lucy's voice was by far the loudest – and this time she could shout just as noisily as she wanted.

"Come on Titch!" yelled Lucy and Joe together.

"Hurry up Curly!" called Jessie.

The pigs ran neck and neck. The noise was deafening as everyone cheered for their favourite pig. Champion was first, but then Curly put his snout just ahead.

Tank passed them both but then he slowed down, letting Shades overtake. Suddenly from the back, Titch dashed forward into the lead.

"Titch is the winner!" shouted Lucy.

"Hurray!" yelled Joe.

Now it was Jessie who felt sad.

"Cheer up Jessie," said Dad. "Piggy racing is just for fun.
And it's not always the biggest one who wins."

"I know," said Jessie, bravely.

"Who wants an ice cream after all that cheering?"
asked Mum.

"We do!" shouted Jessie and Joe.

"Mum, could I have my ice cream now?" asked Lucy.

"Yes, of course," said Lucy's mum. "And I'll have one too. This farm visit has been so much fun!"

Later, Jessie and Joe helped Wilf take the happy pigs back to the pen.

It was the cows' milking time, so Dad and Rocket had already gone to bring them in.

Wash
your han
please.

Before tea, Jessie and Joe went to feed the animals in
Pets' Corner.

"I know you didn't mean to cheat when we raced with
Lucy," said Jessie to Joe, "and I'm glad your pig won."

"Thanks Jessie," said Joe. "*You* can cheer for Titch next
time we have a Piggy Race at Little Oak Farm!"

Top Playground

Long Field

Great Field

Orchard

Tractor Trail

Cows' Field

Stables

Pig Run

Sheep

Lower
Playground

Tractor
Race

Car Park

Ticket Office
and Gift Shop

Toilets

Visitors'
Entrance

Herb
Garden

Café

Little Oak

Milking
Shed

Play Barn and
Fun Room

Dairy

Farmyard

Farmhouse

Pets'
Corner

Ducks'
Pond

Hen
Houses

Sharing Books From Birth to Five

Zoo Patterns

£3.99

0 00 136130 9

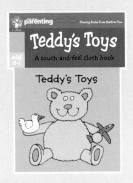

Teddy's Toys

£3.99

0 00 136132 5

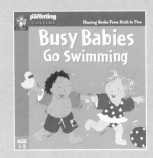

Busy Babies Go Swimming

£3.99

0 00 136139 2

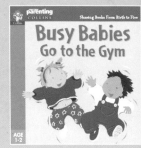

Busy Babies Go to the Gym

£3.99

0 00 136137 6

AGE 0–1

AGE 1–2

Tiny Trumpet

£3.99

0 00 136147 3

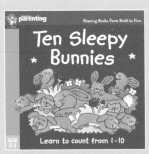

Ten Sleepy Bunnies

£3.99

0 00 136171 6

Rocket to the Rescue

£3.99

0 00 136151 1

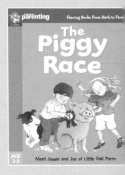

The Piggy Race

£3.99

0 00 136153 8

AGE 2–3

AGE 3–5

The Practical Parenting books are available from all good bookshops and can be ordered direct from HarperCollins Publishers by ringing 0141 7723200 and through the HarperCollins website: www.fireandwater.com

You can also order any of these titles, with free post and packaging, from the Practical Parenting Bookshop on 01326 569339 or send your cheque or postal order together with your name and address to: Practical Parenting Bookshop, Freepost, PO Box 11, Falmouth, TR10 9EN.